Shh!
Can you
keep a secret?

You're about to meet the
Ballet Bunnies, who live hidden
at Millie's ballet school.

Are you ready?

Tiptoe this
way. . . .

Meet the Ballet Bunnies

Dolly

You'll never meet
a bunny who
loves to dance as
much as Dolly.

Fifi

If you're in
trouble, Fifi is
always ready to
lend a helping paw!

Pod

Pod loves to build things out of the bits and pieces he finds. He also loves his tutu!

Trixie

Yawn! When she's not dancing, Trixie likes curling up and having a nice snooze.

For Yumi

This is a work of fiction. Names, characters, places, and incidents either are the product of the author's imagination or are used fictitiously. Any resemblance to actual persons, living or dead, events, or locales is entirely coincidental.

Text copyright © 2020 by Swapna Reddy
Cover art and interior illustrations copyright © 2020 by Binny Talib

All rights reserved. Published in the United States by Random House Children's Books, a division of Penguin Random House LLC, New York. Originally published in paperback by Oxford University Press, Oxford, in 2020.

Random House and the colophon are registered trademarks and A Stepping Stone Book and the colophon are trademarks of Penguin Random House LLC.

Visit us on the Web!
rhcbooks.com

Educators and librarians, for a variety of teaching tools, visit us at
RHTeachersLibrarians.com

Library of Congress Cataloging-in-Publication Data is available upon request.
ISBN 978-0-593-30492-1 (pbk.) — ISBN 978-0-593-30493-8 (lib. bdg.) —
ISBN 978-0-593-30494-5 (ebook)

Printed in the United States of America.
10 9 8 7 6 5 4 3 2
First American Edition 2021

This book has been officially leveled by using the
F&P Text Level Gradient™ Leveling System.

Ballet Bunnies

The New Class

By Swapna Reddy

Illustrated by Binny Talib

A STEPPING STONE BOOK™

Random House 🏠 New York

Chapter 1

Millie had been dreaming of going to Miss Luisa's School of Dance for months now. So, on her sixth birthday, when Mom surprised her with ballet lessons as a gift, she screamed so loudly with joy that she woke up the neighbor's dog.

Today was Millie's first lesson.

She spotted a gold sign for her ballet class and ran her fingers over the swirly writing. She hurried toward the studio, unable to stop the wide grin stretching across her face. This was it. All of Millie's dreams were about to come true. She pushed hard on the door.

"Watch it!" a voice screeched as the wooden door swung open.

A girl in a pink leotard and matching tutu was sitting on the floor and pulling on her ballet shoes. She glared at Millie.

"I'm sorry," Millie apologized. "I didn't see you."

The girl stood and crossed her arms.

"*You're* in the wrong class," she said, scowling.

"I don't think so," Millie said. She looked around the room, confused. "I'm here for ballet too."

Before either girl could say any more, a teacher called all the children together.

"Come along, Amber," she said loudly to the girl in pink.

"Yes, Miss Luisa," Amber replied, her voice now sunny and bright.

Millie followed and watched as Amber took a place by the wooden barre in the middle of the studio. Millie had seen a barre in the ballet book she'd borrowed from the

library. It helped dancers balance while they learned new steps.

Millie copied the others and squeezed her feet into her ballet slippers, wiggling her toes. She tapped her sateen feet on the shiny floor and hopped from foot to foot. An excited giggle bubbled up from her tummy as she looked down at her special shoes.

"Children, we have a new student," Miss Luisa said as she nodded at Millie. "This is Millie."

Millie loved the way Miss Luisa said her name. It sounded like each letter was dancing to a twinkly melody.

"Hi!" Millie waved to the class, beaming at each child staring at her.

But no one waved back.

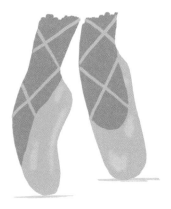

Chapter 2

Miss Luisa led Millie toward the wooden barre, and Millie joined the line of dancers.

"First position, everyone," Miss Luisa said. She clapped her hands.

First position! Millie had seen this on a video. Pushing back her shoulders, Millie stuck out her chin and planted her heels firmly on the floor before pointing her feet outward.

"Watch how Will does it," Miss Luisa said. She pointed to the boy near Millie. "He'll show you."

Millie looked down at her feet and then down at Will's. She couldn't see what she was doing wrong. They *almost* looked the same.

"Come on, Millie," Miss Luisa said.

The way Miss Luisa said Millie's name was no longer twinkly and melodious.

Suddenly, the doors to the studio swung open and in ran a girl with a rainbow tutu and pink hair.

"I'm sorry I'm late, Miss Luisa," the girl yelled. She ran to the barre, skidding across the floor and sliding to a stop on her knee.

Millie smiled as she watched the girl clamber to her feet and take a bow.

"Find your place, Samira," Miss Luisa said.

Samira grinned at Millie, but Amber pulled Samira close as soon as she noticed Millie looking their way.

"Now bend into a plié, children," Miss Luisa said.

What is a plié? Millie wondered.

Millie watched the others rise up and down and tried to join in.

"Very nice, Amber," Miss Luisa said. "Excellent job, Will."

Millie copied Will and moved up and down in time with him.

"Not exactly, Millie," said Miss Luisa. "Why don't you start again with first position?"

Millie stopped. Her shoulders sagged forward as she turned out her feet. She sighed as she saw the others bob up and down without her. They held their arms high over their heads with their chins pointing out. They all looked like ballet dancers. *Real* ballet dancers.

All of them except Millie.

⊙ ✳ ⊙

Millie was relieved when the class ended. She just wanted Mom.

The others disappeared quickly. Soon, she was the last one waiting in the studio.

Millie slumped down on the floor and started to rub her sore toes. Then she heard a tiny voice.

She looked up. No one was there.

"Hello?" Millie called out.

A tiny shadow darted toward a curtained stage at the end of the studio.

"Hello?" Millie called again.

There was no answer.

Millie got to her feet. She dashed over to the stage, where she saw the shadow whiz past again.

"Who's there?" she asked, grabbing the curtain and yanking it back. She gasped. "What is this?"

Chapter 3

"Stay still! She might not have seen us."

There, on the stage, amid a pile of old ballet slippers and discarded tutus, were four little bunny rabbits standing as still as statues.

"How long do we stay still?"

Four TALKING bunnies!

"Just stay still!"

"But I'm stuck in arabesque. I'm not sure how much longer I can hold this."

"I *can* hear you, you know," Millie said.

"Oh, bunny fluff!" one of the bunnies sighed. "You aren't going to scream, are you? Because that's what always happens in the movies."

"It's true," another bunny piped up. "When humans see something they don't understand in the movies, they scream, and then the thing they don't understand screams back. And then the humans scream

17

again, and they all scream because everyone feels terrified."

"All I feel is hungry for ice cream," Millie confessed.

The bunnies giggled, their furry bellies jiggling, and Millie laughed with them.

"I told you she was a good one," another bunny announced smugly to the others.

Millie reached out her hand, and the tallest of the group jumped onto it.

"Who *are* you?" Millie asked. She raised her palm so that she and the bunny were nose to nose. "*What* are you?"

"I'm Fifi," the bunny said, resting her paws on her hips. "And we are the Ballet Bunnies."

A golden-colored bunny spun forward in perfect circles and curtsied. "I'm Dolly."

The bunny with a tuft of glossy black fur hanging over his eye, stuck out his paw, and

Millie shook it very gently. "I'm Pod," he said.

The tiniest bunny let out a yawn and took Millie's outstretched hand next. "I'm Trixie," she said as Millie tickled her softly under her chin.

Millie climbed carefully onto the stage. She looked at the piles of ballet shoes that had been stacked and filled with balled-up pom-poms to make a row of beds. Tutus had been laid delicately over the slippers like fluffy bedcovers.

She sat back on her feet. "I'm Millie, by the way."

"We know," Dolly said. She hopped up Millie's arm all the way to her shoulder. "We saw you in class today."

Dolly spun three perfect pirouettes down Millie's other arm.

"How did you do that?" Millie asked, amazed. "I've tried to do pirouettes at home, but I keep falling over."

Fifi leapt forward and pirouetted alongside Dolly. "We can show you if you want."

"Yes, please," Millie said. She watched carefully as Pod joined in.

She stood in a clear spot on the stage as the bunnies talked her through the spin.

"You're doing it, Millie!" Trixie cried.

"I am!" Millie spun perfect circles, trying not to lose her focus. Then she tumbled back onto a pile of leotards, and the bunnies rushed to her.

"I felt like a real dancer!" Millie smiled at

Trixie as Fifi, Pod, and Dolly danced around them.

The sudden creak of the studio door swinging open stopped the bunnies in their tracks.

"Millie?" a voice called loudly.

It was Mom!

Chapter 4

"I have to go!" Millie said, jumping up at the sound of her mom's voice.

"Will we see you next week?" Fifi called after her.

Millie hadn't even thought about returning to class. Ballet was difficult—more difficult than she could have imagined—and she wasn't sure she'd ever make any friends in her class.

But as Millie looked at the friendly little rabbits next to the ballet slippers and tutus, she felt torn.

"There you are!" Mom exclaimed as she came into the studio.

Millie leapt off the stage. She whipped the curtain after her, hoping to shield the little bunnies from her mother.

"Mom!" Millie cried.

"I'm sorry I'm late, darling," Mom said, rushing to grab Millie's backpack. Millie's eyes widened as she spotted Dolly jumping into the very same backpack.

"I've got it!" Millie said, diving for the bag before Mom could get it.

⊙ ✳ ⊙

On the way home, Millie couldn't concentrate on anything but the little rabbit in her bag.

"Tell me about your class," Mom said. "Did you make any friends?"

Millie wrinkled her nose. "Not really," she said.

"It's still early," Mom replied.

Mom told Millie about her own dance classes as a child and how she wished she hadn't had to give them up. Millie tried to listen and nodded along, but her tummy bubbled with excitement every time she felt a little nudge from her bag. She wrapped both her hands over a strap and gave it a tiny tug to remind Dolly she was still there.

"Is your bag too heavy?" Mom asked, reaching out a hand.

"No, Mom," Millie said, releasing her hands. "It's as light as bunny fluff."

Dolly laughed from inside the bag, and Millie had to pretend to cough to cover up the tiny giggle.

Chapter 5

As soon as she and Mom got home, Millie raced upstairs to her room. She delicately laid down her backpack on her bed, unzipping and opening up the bag.

The little Ballet Bunny hopped out, stretching her front legs.

"Dolly!" Millie said. "What were you thinking?"

"Oh, bunny fluff! Sorry, Millie," Dolly replied. "You didn't say if you were coming to class next week, and I just had to know."

She jumped into Millie's palm, peering around the bedroom. "I've left the studio sometimes to see the recitals at the old town theater, but I've never been in a real bedroom before," she squealed.

Millie smiled at the little bunny. "Welcome to my room."

Dolly squeaked with joy and spun a perfect pirouette. She sprang around the room, marveling at Millie's collection of ballet books and tutus. She flipped open a music box and whirled in time with the tiny ballerina figurine inside.

Millie laughed as Dolly danced with her ribbons and held up Millie's hair bow clips against her silky ears.

"Dinnertime, Millie," Mom called up from the kitchen. "It's noodles—your favorite."

"I'll be right down," Millie called back.

"Dinner?" Dolly said, raising an eyebrow. She cocked her head to one side. "Did I hear your mom mention noodles?"

"You want noodles?" Millie asked, confused. "Do bunnies even eat noodles?"

"This Ballet Bunny does," Dolly said with a grin.

Chapter 6

"Can I go to my room, Mom?"
Millie asked as she gobbled up the last of her
meal. She hid some of the noodles and green
beans in her pockets for Dolly. "I really want
to practice what I learned today."

Mom nodded and waved her out of the
kitchen.

Millie sprinted up to her bedroom to find that Dolly was no longer dancing around. Instead, the little bunny was sitting in front of the mirror and was covered from the tips of her ears to the bottom of her fluffy tail in Millie's hair bow clips.

"What do you think?" Dolly asked. "Is it too much?"

Millie giggled and removed three bows

from Dolly's back and two from her tail. "That's better," she said, and Dolly gave a twirl.

Millie found her old tea set. She placed the noodles and beans that she'd saved into one of the little cups and set it on the floor. She turned a small sugar bowl upside down as a seat for Dolly.

"Stir-fried noodles," Dolly said between mouthfuls. "They're my favorite."

Millie chuckled. "Mine too!"

Dolly finished her food and hopped up onto Millie's bed. She twirled with a length of purple velvet ribbon that hung from the post of the bed. She wrapped herself in the soft fabric.

"How does it feel when you dance, Millie?" the bunny asked.

Millie sat down, leaned against the edge of her bed, and shut her eyes.

"It makes me feel happy," Millie said. "And when I jump, I feel like I'm flying through clouds of—"

"Cotton candy?" Dolly finished.

"Yes! That's it," Millie said. "Like I'm in a world of cotton candy, light and floaty and—"

"Happy?" Dolly said.

"Exactly!"

"I feel the same way," Dolly said. She jumped down and landed in Millie's lap. "And there's no other feeling like it."

Millie and Dolly danced around the room, practicing their pirouettes and pliés. Dolly helped Millie turn out her feet just like Miss Luisa had said to in class.

Before they knew it, Mom came in to turn out the lights for bedtime. Dolly quickly jumped out of sight, reappearing only after Millie's mom had left the room.

"I had so much fun dancing with you today," Millie said. She pulled the bedcovers over Dolly.

"Me too." Dolly smiled. "It's just like cotton candy." She yawned. "Sharing cotton candy with others is always more fun than getting sticky whiskers all on your own."

Millie hugged Dolly close, and they both drifted off to a sleep full of pirouettes and the lightest cotton candy.

◦ ✳ ◦

Millie woke the next morning to a fluffy tail in her face. Tiny, snoring Dolly was stretched out next to her.

"You should get back to the studio,"

Millie said, waking the bunny gently. "The others might be worried."

Dolly's silky ears bobbed in agreement. "Are you coming back next week?" Dolly asked.

Millie felt a heavy feeling in her tummy as she remembered the lesson with Miss Luisa and Amber and Will. But watching Dolly reminded Millie of their cotton candy world, and the heavy feeling started to lift.

Millie nodded. "I'll be there," she said.

Dolly smiled. Then she jumped through the open window, off the window ledge, and onto the hammock strung up in the yard.

"Will you be okay?" Millie called after Dolly.

"I'll be fine," Dolly said. "It's the same route home as it was from the theater."

Millie waved goodbye, and the little bunny hurried off through the gap in the garden gate and back home.

Chapter 7

It had been a week since Millie had attended Miss Luisa's School of Dance.

She'd thought of nothing else but the Ballet Bunnies. But now, back in the studio, she felt farther away from them than ever before. She had to get through this lesson to see Fifi, Trixie, Pod, and Dolly again—but as she watched Will land perfect sautés one after another, she wondered if she could.

Millie slid on her ballet shoes and joined the others.

"Children, today you will be working

in pairs," Miss Luisa said, tapping the barre. "Samira, you will work with Will. And, Amber, you will work with Millie."

Millie felt like her stomach dropped right through the floor of the studio.

"But, Miss Luisa," Amber began in her

sweetest voice, "Millie can't even do a basic *first position*. I wouldn't want her to hold me back."

Millie hung her head. She'd practiced all week, remembering the advice Dolly had given her. Amber's words made her feel like her feet were glued to the ground and her arms were made of lead. She held on tight to the little bunny's words of encouragement.

"I've been practicing, Miss Luisa," Millie said. She forced out her feet just like Dolly had shown her and demonstrated a perfect first position.

"Very good, Millie!" Miss Luisa said, raising an eyebrow at Amber.

Before Amber could say anything back, Miss Luisa started the class.

"Face your partner, children," Miss Luisa said. "Imagine you are their reflection. Mirror their moves."

Millie watched Will and Samira. Will flung his arm high, and Samira matched it. He lifted his leg, and Samira copied. Millie smiled. It was like magic. It looked as if an invisible string connected them.

"You're supposed to be facing *me*," Amber barked at Millie.

Millie took a deep breath and faced Amber.

At the exact same time, Amber threw out her arm over the barre and Millie bent her legs.

"Girls!" Miss Luisa said, shaking her head. "You need to mirror *each other.*"

"Yes, Miss Luisa," Amber said with a bright smile.

She whipped her head around to face Millie. "*You're* supposed to be following *me.*"

"Why can't you follow me?" Millie asked.

"Because you don't know anything about ballet," Amber retorted. She jumped up into a sauté.

"Come on," Amber said meanly.

Both Amber and Millie prepared to sauté. But as they took off, Amber switched the move, spinning into a pirouette in the air.

Millie mirrored Amber, but her legs locked
around each other and she crashed to the
floor, knocking against the barre.

"Millie!" Miss Luisa cried. "Concentrate, please."

Amber laughed and got ready to jump again, but Millie didn't bother to copy her

this time. Will laughed along with Amber as Millie clambered to her feet. Tears streamed down her face as she ran across the studio to the bathroom, as far away from the ballet class as she could get.

Chapter 8

"Millie?"

Dolly, Trixie, Fifi, and Pod hopped across the floor of the girls' bathroom, following the sounds of sobs.

"I won't go back," Millie cried. "I won't."

The four bunnies crawled under the door of the farthest bathroom stall, where they found Millie on the floor, hugging her knees as she cried.

"Oh, Millie," Fifi said. "That Amber was rotten to you."

Dolly hopped up over Millie's foot and landed on her knees. She nuzzled her way under Millie's downturned head and squished her face into Millie's, gently licking away her tears.

Millie dropped her chin down to her chest. "I'm just not good enough."

"Bunny fluff," Fifi said. "Yes, you are."

"I can't keep up with the others," Millie said, her voice small.

Dolly jumped into Millie's hand. "But you don't have to, Millie. It's okay to go at your own pace," she said gently.

"This is only your second lesson," Pod agreed. "Amber has been coming here since she was tiny—"

"Maybe even tinier than me," Trixie piped up, getting a giggle out of Millie.

"It's true," Dolly said with a kind smile. "You'll be dancing like the others with more lessons. Remember why you love dancing. Remember the cotton candy."

Millie wiped away the tears on her face. She'd made up her mind.

"You're right," she sniffed. "I *do* love dancing. But I would rather just keep dancing at home." Millie wrapped her arms around herself. "That way I don't have to deal with Amber."

The bunnies looked at one another, their shoulders slumped and their wide eyes shiny with tears.

"But we will miss you so much, Millie!" Fifi cried. Dolly ran out of the bathroom.

"And I'll miss you too," Millie said. Her

chest ached as though her heart was being pulled in half.

She scooped up Fifi, Pod, and Trixie. She kissed each of them gently on the head and held them close.

"Where's Dolly?" Millie asked, looking for

the fourth bunny. "I can't go without saying goodbye to her. I just can't!"

Fifi, Pod, and Trixie hurried down, searching each stall for Dolly.

"Dolly?" Fifi called out.

"I'm here," Dolly said, reappearing.

"Oh, Dolly!" Millie cried. "I'm so glad you came back."

Dolly hopped over to Millie's open palm and nuzzled it reassuringly. She then carefully placed a tiny object into Millie's hand.

Millie peered at her palm. "What's this, Dolly?"

"It's for you," the bunny replied. "I want

you to have something to remember us by."

Millie picked up the tiny object. It was a strip of a soft pink tutu, rolled up and fastened to the end of one of Millie's hair clips.

"It looks like cotton candy!" Millie said, hugging the bunny close.

Millie looked in the mirror before sliding the clip into her hair. She gazed down at the bunnies as she touched the rosy fabric. Millie remembered how

they had pirouetted together on the stage
when they had first met and how much fun
they'd had.

Chapter 9

The bathroom door rattled, and the bunnies jumped out of sight.

Millie turned to see Samira come into the bathroom and then smile kindly at her.

"I thought what Amber did today was really unfair," Samira said.

Millie looked at the floor, unable to meet Samira's gaze.

Samira squatted down to look up at Millie. "She can be mean sometimes," Samira said softly.

"It doesn't matter," Millie said, sticking out her chin. "I'm not sure I'm coming back here again anyway."

"Really?" Samira asked.

Millie shook her head. "You're all way ahead of me."

"Yeah, because we've been here for aaaages," Samira said, pulling Millie to stand next to her. "This is your second lesson, and I saw your first position was looking really good."

Millie felt a warm feeling in her chest. "I've been working on that all week."

"It really shows," Samira encouraged her.

Samira stuck out her feet into first position. From the corner of her eye, Millie spotted Dolly hiding behind the trash can. Dolly stuck her feet into first position, too, and nodded to Millie to do the same.

Then Samira switched to second position, and Millie followed.

"Miss Luisa would love your posture," Samira said. "She's always telling me to straighten my neck like a giraffe." She relaxed her feet and stretched her neck forward. "Do I look like a giraffe, Millie?"

Millie chuckled. "You're the best giraffe I've ever met in the bathroom."

The girls straightened out their necks and walked around, each doing her best impression of a giraffe. When Samira tried to pirouette as a giraffe, she knocked into Millie, and the two tumbled to the floor in a giggling heap. Dolly was right. Dancing with others was definitely more fun than dancing on your own.

"I wish you weren't leaving," Samira said

to Millie. "I was going to ask if we could be partners next time."

Millie sat up and stared at Samira. "You want *me* to be *your* partner?" she said, astounded.

"If you don't mind," Samira said, squeezing in closer to Millie and giving her a friendly nudge.

"I'd love that!" Millie grinned. She had made a friend.

"I love your hair clip," Samira said, tilting her head to admire the tiny pin. "It looks like a ball of cotton candy! I love cotton candy."

"Me too," said Millie.

"I especially like dressing up as cotton candy," Samira said.

Millie giggled as Samira pretended to nibble at her fluffy tutu.

"I hope you don't leave, Millie," Samira said. She stood up and hopscotched to the bathroom door and back toward the studio.

Millie watched the door swing shut. The bunnies scrambled out of their hiding places.

What Dolly had said stuck out in Millie's

mind. Maybe it didn't matter that she wasn't as good as the other dancers. Maybe all that mattered was that it was more fun to enjoy dancing with others.

"I don't want you to leave, Millie," Dolly

pleaded, looking up at Millie. "Please say you'll come back."

Dancing like a giraffe with Samira had filled Millie's tummy with that warm, happy feeling of flying through clouds of cotton candy—the feeling that Millie usually only got from dancing. Now that she and Samira would be partners, Millie couldn't help but think that every week might be a cotton candy week.

She took a breath. "You know what?" Millie said, beaming at the bunnies. "I think I will."

"Sticky whiskers for everyone!" Fifi cheered as Millie scooped up the Ballet Bunnies into the biggest, fluffiest hug.

Basic ballet moves

First position

Second position

Third
position

Fourth
position

Fifth position

Glossary of ballet terms

Arabesque—Standing on one leg, the dancer extends the other leg out behind them.

Barre—A horizontal bar at waist level on which ballet dancers rest a hand for support during certain exercises.

Demi-plié—A small bend of the knees, with heels kept on the floor.

En pointe—Dancing on the very tips of the toes.

Grand plié—A large bend of the knees, with heels raised off the floor.

Pas de deux—A dance for two people.

Pirouette—A spin made on one foot, turning all the way around.

Plié—A movement in which the dancer bends the knees and straightens them again while feet are turned out and heels are kept on the floor.

Relevé—A movement in which the dancer rises on the tips of the toes.

Sauté—A jump off both feet, landing in the same position.

Twirl and spin with
the Ballet Bunnies
in their next adventure!

Ballet Bunnies

Let's Dance

By Swapna Reddy   Illustrated by Binny Talib

Discover more magic in these page-turning adventures!

For the totally
unique ballerina!

For the
unicorn-obsessed!

For dog lovers
and budding pirates!

For cat lovers and
wannabe mermaids!